Hi and Lois

By Mort Walker and Dik Browne

TOR

A Tom Doherty Associates Book

**Copyright 1983
by King Features Syndicate, Inc.
All Rights Reserved
ISBN: 49-076-3**

A Tom Doherty Associates Original

**Printed in the United States of America
Distributed by Pinnacle Books, Inc.**

A LIGHT SWITCH THAT DOESN'T TURN ANYTHING OFF OR ON...
CLICK! CLICK

AND A RADIO KNOB THAT'S ALWAYS FALLING OFF...

A CORNER OF A RUG THAT WON'T LIE FLAT

A BROKEN LAMP WITH THE BROKEN PART FACING THE WALL...

A JOHN THAT KEEPS RUNNING UNLESS YOU JIGGLE THE HANDLE...

A FURNACE THAT THUMPS IN THE NIGHT...
THUMP THUMP THUMP
WHO'S THERE?

TABLES THAT WOBBLE... CHAIRS THAT CREAK... BEDS THAT SQUEAK... AND A PHONE THAT RINGS THE MINUTE YOU GET IN THE TUB...
THEN YOU DON'T HAVE A HOUSE, YOU HAVE A HOME

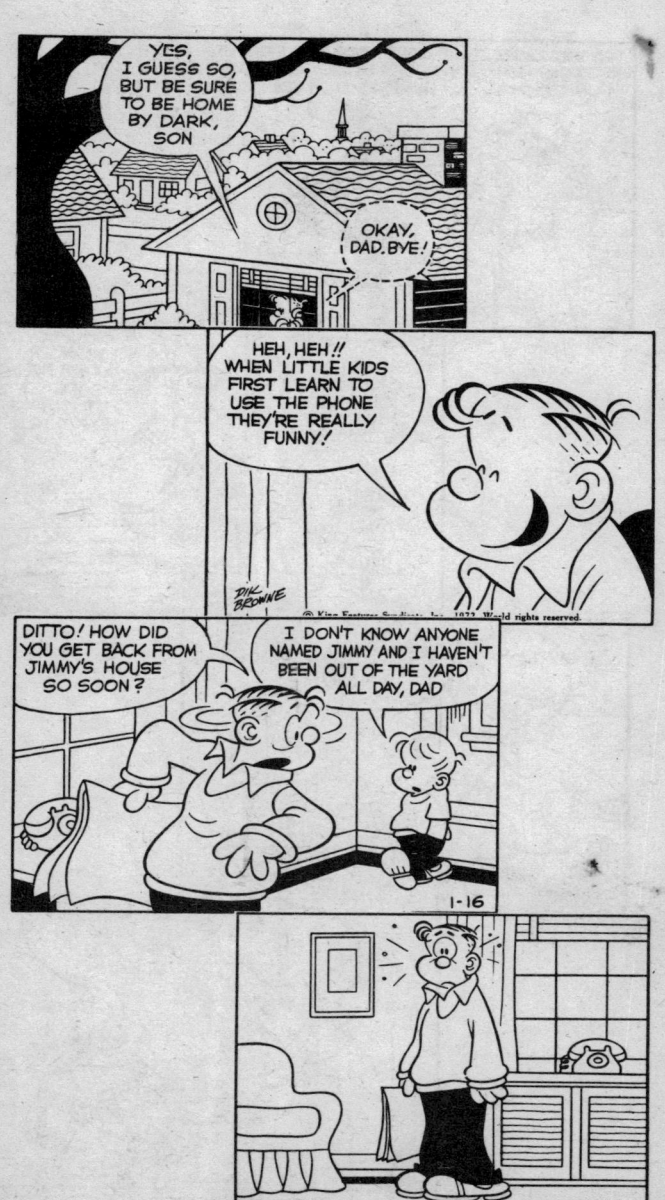

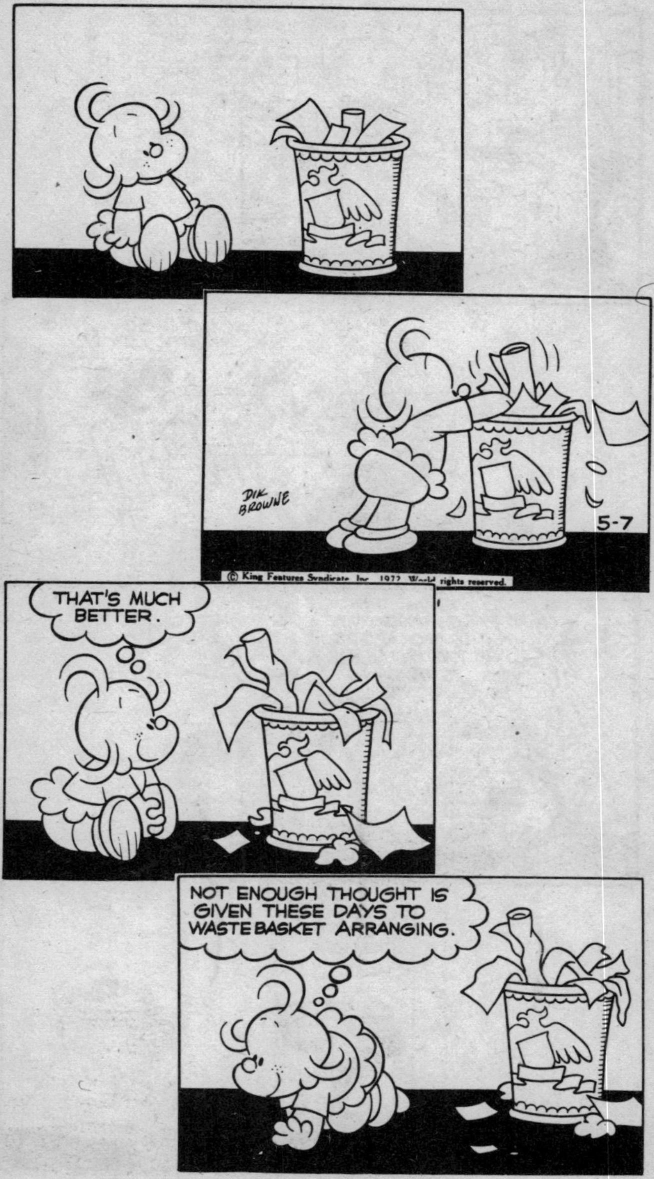